Kamik
Joins the Pack

Published by Inhabit Media Inc. • www.inhabitmedia.com

Inhabit Media Inc. (Iqaluit), P.O. Box 11125, Iqaluit, Nunavut, X0A 1H0
(Toronto), 191 Eglinton Avenue East, Suite 301, Toronto, M4P 1K1

Editors: Neil Christopher and Kelly Ward
Art Director: Danny Christopher

This project was made possible in part by the Government of Canada.

We acknowledge the support of the Canada Council for the Arts for our publishing program.

ISBN: 978-1-77227-125-6

Library and Archives Canada Cataloguing in Publication

Baker, Darryl, author
        Kamik joins the pack / adapted from the memories of
Darryl Baker; illustrated by Qin Leng.

ISBN 978-1-77227-125-6 (paperback)

        1. Sled dogs--Juvenile fiction. 2. Sled dogs--Training--
Juvenile fiction. I. Leng, Qin, illustrator II. Title.

PS8603.A4525K36 2016   jC813'.6   C2016-904803-9

Printed in Canada

Kamik
Joins the Pack

Adapted from the memories of **Darryl Baker** · Illustrated by **Qin Leng**

Kamik ran beside Jake as they made their way down the snowy road toward Jake's uncle's house.

Jake was excited to show his uncle how much his puppy had learned and how obedient he was becoming. Jake's uncle was a great musher, who had won many dogsled races.

"Try to look extra strong and obedient today," Jake said as he looked down at his puppy.

Kamik just wagged his tail and walked on.

"Hello, Jake!" Jake's uncle called as he looked up from his work. Kamik ran and sat next to him, waiting to be patted. "Your puppy is getting bigger!" he said, as he gave Kamik a tap on the head.

"He is!" Jake said, feeling a bit of pride. "I am already teaching him commands to turn. He is very smart. I can't wait to get more dogs so that Kamik can lead my very own dog team."

Jake's uncle was just beginning to harness his team. The dogs all looked very excited and eager to run. Jake imagined Kamik as the lead dog of the team. He was sure Kamik could lead the fastest dog team around!

5

"It is good that Kamik is smart," Jake's uncle said as he continued to harness his dogs. "Smart, hard-working dogs are the best dogs. Being a good musher takes a lot of work."

"I know," Jake said. "I have to give the dogs lots of exercise, right?"

"That is true. But before you take out a dog team, you must make sure they are healthy and in good condition," Jake's uncle replied.

"In the fall and winter, I have to cut my dogs' nails so they will not break while they're running. I must also check to make sure no ice has formed in the hair on the bottoms of their paws. And they need to be fed every day—even in the middle of a blizzard, when you may not feel like going outside to feed them. Dogs rely on us to keep them healthy so that they don't get hurt when they are running with the pack."

Jake watched as his uncle checked all his dogs, lifting their paws and inspecting them. Jake had never checked Kamik's paws. He leaned down and lifted Kamik's front paw, just as his uncle was doing.

"There are lots of other skills that come in handy, too," Jake's uncle continued. "Dogs love to chew on harnesses and ropes, so it helps to know how to sew and braid in order to fix those. And you'll need to know how to build doghouses and fix your sled if it breaks."

"Wow," said Jake, "I didn't know there would be so much to do." Jake looked down at the snow. He did not know how to do many of these things.

Jake's uncle put a hand on his shoulder. "You don't need to learn everything all at once," he said with a smile. "You can learn alongside your dogs.

"When I was your age, I had five dogs. They did not know how to pull a sled, but one day I harnessed them and tried to ride around town. The dogs would not pull the sled, so I had to get off and walk with them most of the way home. I was sweating from pulling my dogs along, even though it was the middle of winter. When I was halfway home, some mushers passed me with their dog teams. I felt so embarrassed, but I never gave up! From that day I started to slowly learn what I needed to know to build a dog team."

Thinking about his uncle at his own age made
Jake feel a little bit better.

"So what should I do first?" Jake asked. "My *ataatasiaq* told me to spend lots
of time with Kamik to get to know him, and my *anaanatsiaq* taught me how to
teach him commands while I play with him."

"Your grandparents taught you well. Dogs and their masters do need to spend
a lot of time together in order to understand each other. My dogs know
when I'm happy and when I'm upset. To know for sure if Kamik
can be a lead dog, he needs to run with other dogs."

16

"I let new dogs run at the back of the team to see how they behave. Just like people, dogs behave in different ways. Some dogs work very hard when they pull. They look straight ahead as they run and never bother the other dogs. Some dogs are not as hard-working. They look around or back at me while they're running and bother the other dogs. A lead dog needs to be very focused," Jake's uncle said as he harnessed another of his dogs.

There was one empty harness left at the back of the team. Jake looked at Kamik. He knew Kamik could be a hard-working dog, and he wanted so badly to see him run with his uncle's team.

"Maybe we should see how Kamik does with the team?" Jake's uncle offered.

"Yes!" Jake said, barely able to contain his excitement.

Jake grabbed the harness and slid it onto Kamik's back. Jake's uncle showed him how to attach Kamik to the lead and Kamik stood in line with the other dogs, eager and ready to run.

19

"We won't be able to go very far with Kamik his first time pulling. Puppies can only run for a mile or two at first. Pulling is hard work and we don't want to strain his muscles," Jake's uncle said.

Jake nodded, before leaning down to check Kamik's harness one last time. "Okay, boy," he whispered to his puppy, "time to show us you can lead."

Kamik lifted his head and licked at Jake's face.

Jake climbed onto the sled with his uncle. He could hardly believe Kamik was about to run with a dog team for the first time.

"Are you ready?" Jake's uncle asked him. Jake smiled and nodded as the sound of the whip started the dogs running.

As the dogs took off, Kamik ran hard and fast with the rest of the pack, never looking back.

Contributors

Darryl Baker is a teacher in Arviat, Nunavut. He was born in Churchill, Manitoba, and raised in Arviat. In 2006 Darryl graduated from the Nunavut Teacher Education Program, along with other Inuit from the same community, and he has been teaching at the Levi Angmak Elementary School since. Besides his career as a teacher, he enjoys dog mushing and has been an active participant in Hudson Bay Quest and other dog team races between Rankin and Arviat. He started raising dogs as a young man, picking up interest from his late brother-in-law, Bernie Sulurayok. As a young boy, he often went hunting for seals at the floe edge with his brother-in-law. He eventually started raising dogs on his own, spending quality time with them and bonding strongly, gaining respect. Today he is still actively mushing and hopes to pass it on to his twin boys.

Qin Leng was born in Shanghai, China, and lived in France and Montreal, Quebec. She now lives and works as a designer and illustrator in Toronto, Ontario. Her father, an artist himself, was a great influence on her. She grew up surrounded by paintings, and it became second nature for her to express herself through art. She graduated from the Mel Hoppenheim School of Cinema and has received many awards for her animated short films and artwork. Qin has always loved to illustrate the innocence of children and has developed a passion for children's books. She has illustrated numerous picture books for publishers in Canada, the United States, and South Korea.